The Iron Heel

"[The Iron Heel] serves up food for thought with an appealing heart-on-sleeve warmth. You may well find yourself humming some of those tunes on the way out."

Elisabeth Vincentelli
The New York Times

"The production manages to give the story a deeper emotional impact thanks to the terrific cast...But most of all, the production brings alive the hope and horror of the revolutionaries who fought in the early 20th century in a way that feels relevant and contemporary to a modern audience."

Geoff Bailey
Socialist Workers

"Edward Einhorn not only absorbed creatively the impetus given by Jack London's The Iron Heel but also thought over again in its light political discourse as a whole."

Alexandra Scaggs
The Financial Times

5 STARS "This well-acted, cleverly executed production is a mind-bending tour de force of ideas, as only Einhorn can deliver, with darkly twisting humor and swaths of realism thrown in to perplex."

Carole DiTosti
blogcritics

"A rousing tale of rigged elections, false identities, prison escapes, bombings, romantic interludes, songs of solidarity, and scenes of terrifying carnage."

Ethan Kanfer
ethankanfer.com

"I was impressed by how moved much of the audience was - old lefties and younger millennials finding a common bond in a story and songs over 100 years old. It is a fun night."

Scott Mitchell
What's On Off-Broadway

"Einhorn and his Untitled Theater Company #61 prove again a master (but a benevolent one) in turning intellectual matters into engaging stage shows."

Jonathan Mandell
New York Theater

"A solid introduction to Jack London and his work in a time wrought with doubts about the current economic and political landscape across the globe. Einhorn's adaptation is a testament to the idea that, sometimes, the best way to understand the past is the best way to understand the present. "

Sarah Weber
Theater is Easy

The Iron Heel

Adapted from a book by
Jack London

Adapted by
Edward Einhorn

Theater 61 Press New York

Published by Theater 61 Press
A division of Untitled Theater Company #61
Copyright © Edward Einhorn 2017
Based on the book, *The Iron Heel* © Jack London 1908
"Adaptor's Note", Copyright © Edward Einhorn 2017
Manufactured in the United States of America
ISBN: 978-0-9988735-0-3

Book design by Clinton Corbett

TABLE OF CONTENTS

Yvonne Roen

ADAPTOR'S NOTE

"History doesn't repeat itself, but it often rhymes," as Mark Twain supposedly said. More accurately, that quote belongs to our collective unconscious. It's an idea that sounded so true it had to be put in the mouth of one of our most important satirists. *The Iron Heel*, which many consider the first modern dystopia, is also a satire of sorts—like many dystopias, it is an exaggerated portrayal of our society, of Jack London's America. It was written in 1908, and it was science fiction when it was written, although certain incidents have the ring of historical fact. It predicts World War One, Pearl Harbor, the stock market crash, even the term "the 99 percent" (though, awkwardly, here, it would be the 99.1%, with London preferring mathematical accuracy to pithiness).

In many ways, the novel predicts the dictatorships that will arise throughout the 20th Century. One of the novel's fans, Leon Trotsky, who rightfully called it "prophetic" (when reviewing it in the journal *Art & Revolution*) might have been wise to heed its warnings. But more importantly, it presented a distorted mirror to reality, distorted quite deliberately by Socialist propaganda.

London was a Marxist, and he openly stated that propaganda was his purpose. Thus, though there is a clear connection between his prose and that of Hemingway and Orwell after him, I prefer to make the connection to Brecht's political satires, theatrical parables calculated to outrage the audience about the consequences of unvarnished Capitalism. Like Brecht, my adaptation is consciously theatrical. For its music, it uses revised lyrics to historic folks songs—work and protest songs written mostly after London died, but during the time in which his story is set. It is a show whose naked purpose is to examine political issues, couching them in a story.

London's novel is a fascinating historical text, but of course my deeper interest in it is the way in which the American society of a century ago rhymes so closely with so many of the issues we face today. It is about an election between a Socialist and an Oligarch, shaped by terrorism. It would be too simplistic to say the Oligarch is Trump, or that the Socialist is Sanders. In fact some of Trump's populism (in particular, the fear that immigrants are stealing jobs) might well have resonated with London.

But the issues that are swirling around us now clearly were thick in the air one hundred years ago, and the fear that the United States might descend into Fascism under the wrong leader is one that has returned today. The world isn't repeating, not quite, our world has changed since London died. But the rhymes…they are everywhere.

Edward Einhorn

The Iron Heel

Adapted by
Edward Einhorn

The Iron Heel premiered on July 23, 2016. It played from July 23 – September 5, 2016, at the following venues in New York City: Freedom Socialist Party, Freedom Hall; Governors Island, House 8B (the Dysfunctional Collective); Jackie Robinson Park; Judson Memorial Church; South Oxford Space; West Side Community Garden.

PRODUCTION TEAM

DIRECTOR

Edward Einhorn

STAGE MANAGER

Blake Kile

ASSISTANT DIRECTOR

Becca Silbert

SOUND DESIGN

Chris Chappell

COSTUME/PROPS DESIGN

Ramona Ponce

PRODUCTION ASSISTANTS

Deonna Dolac,
Yael Haskal, and Mark Hunstein

ACTORS

Note: This play is conceived for six actors, three of whom play multiple roles. It is of course possible to use more actors, though the same actor should play WICKSON and the ACTOR.

Craig Anderson..............BISHOP MOREHOUSE, etc
Kevin Argus.....................JOHN CUNNINGHAM, etc
Charles Ouda............................ ERNEST EVERHARD
Yvonne Roen............................ ANTONIA MEREDITH
Victoria Rulle ....AVIS EVERHARD
Trav SD..WICKSON, etc

CAST LIST

ANTONIA MEREDITH – A historian and propagandist, from the 27th Century

AVIS CUNNINGHAM EVERHARD – A young member of the middle class who joins the revolution after meeting her husband, Ernest

ERNEST EVERHARD – A young working class man who becomes a leader of the revolution

ACTOR 1

    ACTOR – Part of the 27th Century acting company; a questioning sort
    HAMMERFELD – A professor of sociology
    WICKSON – The owner of Sierra Mills, a member of the Oligarchy
    MRS. WICKSON – His wife, a socialite
    SOCIALIST 3
    CONDUCTOR
    MAN ON STREET
    CRAZED MAN

CAST LIST (continued)

ACTOR 2

    JOHN CUNNINGHAM – Avis' father, a physics professor

    INGRAM – A lawyer

    JAMES ROBERTS – A Democratic congressional candidate

    BIEDENBACH – A German revolutionary socialist

    GARTHWAITE – A revolutionary in Chicago

    SOCIALIST 2

    DEAD MAN

ACTOR 3

    BISHOP MOREHOUSE – A devout Catholic and friend of AVIS JACKSON – A one-armed working man, injured at the Sierra Mill

    WASHINGTON – A union leader and a sell out

    PARKHURST – A prison doctor and secret socialist

    SOCIALIST 1

Trav SD, Charles Ouda

TIME AND PLACE

The framework is a 27th Century acting company, living in a Socialist utopia, telling a story that happens in an early 20th Century dystopia (centered mostly around San Francisco Bay Area). Note that both the 20th Century story and the 27th Century story were pure science fiction at the time *The Iron Heel* was originally written.

(l to r) Deonna Dolac, Kevin Argus, Charles Ouda, Trav SD, Craig Anderson, Yvonne Roen, Victoria Rulle, Mark Hunstein

Craig Anderson, Trav SD

Charles Ouda, Victoria Rulle

THE IRON HEEL

Adapted by Edward Einhorn
from the book by Jack London

PROLOGUE

(The stage has a large table, around which the actors are gathered, eating. The actors are finishing their dinner. ANTONIA MEREDITH stands. She holds a journal in her hand.)

ANTONIA

My dear comrades, thanks for joining us for this performance. I am Antonia Meredith, a historian and propagandist, and together these actors and I are going to tell you a recently uncovered story, found in a journal almost 700 years old. We're just finishing our dinner, please let us know if you're hungry, we have some rolls left over, and I think a little wine, if anyone wants some. You may notice something about all our clothes, as well as the plates, the glasses, the furniture and everything else here onstage with us. It is all in the style of the twentieth century, which was of course the era of the Oligarchy, also commonly known as the Iron Heel. I see that many of you also dressed for the occasion, which of course we appreciate. An interesting fact about the term "The Iron Heel," which we just recently discovered. It was actually coined by Ernest Everhard, one of the main characters in tonight's drama.

ERNEST

Ernest was the hero of the revolution. It will be my honor to play him this evening.

ANTONIA

He was one of many heroes, I should point out, no one man can change history alone. But heretofore, his story was unknown. And that is just the beginning of what we have learned. This journal, written by Ernest's wife, Avis, is truly an amazing document. Her words have filled in blanks that have puzzled historians like me for centuries.

(She hands the journal to AVIS.)

AVIS

The real journal has become part of the National Collective. Its pages are yellowed and falling apart. But this how the journal looked, 700 years ago.

ANTONIA

It was hiding inside an oak tree, just where Avis placed it in 1932. Perhaps some of you heard about its recent discovery. What we are going to present to you tonight is a historically accurate Reenactment Drama, my specialty as a propagandist. For those of you who have not attended a Reenactment Drama before, the tradition is to have a historian, such as myself, onstage throughout, to help guide you and the actors through the proceedings. Though drama always has a touch of invention, our goal is to present to you the facts, as closely as we can to actual historical events.

ACTOR

Excuse me, but I was wondering—since I know that we invented some of the dialogue, how do we know it is an actual fact?

ANTONIA

It is my job to know the patterns of history, and to inform you of what would most likely have been said.

ACTOR

But we can still improvise?

ANTONIA

As long as you stay within the bounds of historical probability. It is important to remain as accurate as possible, because the most effective propaganda is always based on truth. But feel free to ask me questions throughout, if anything seems unclear. Is there anything else I can clarify?

ACTOR

Just a few background details. While we were
rehearsing, I was a little unclear on how and
when the Oligarchy came to be.

ANTONIA

Avis' story begins in February 1912, and the date
traditionally given to the start of the Iron Heel is
1913. But it is difficult to trace the Oligarchy to a
single moment; as usual it was an accumulation
of growing historical forces. Let me remind you:
in the early twentieth century, Capitalism was
adjudged to be the culmination of bourgeois
rule, the ripened fruit of the bourgeois
revolution. We of today can but applaud that
judgment. Following upon Capitalism, it was
expected that Socialism would emerge. Out of
the decay of self-seeking Capitalism would arise
that flower of the ages. The Brotherhood of Man,
as they called it at the time. In other words, our
current system. What they did not realize was
that the journey would be so treacherous. Too
late did the Socialist movement of the early
twentieth century divine the coming of the
Oligarchy. Even as it was divined, the Oligarchy
was there—a fact established in blood, a
stupendous and awful reality.

> (AVIS rises, clutching her diary. She sits on the
> ground and opens it.)

AVIS

It is so quiet and peaceful, and I sit here, and ponder, and am restless. It is the quiet that makes me restless. It seems unreal. All the world is quiet, but it is the quiet before the storm. I strain my ears, and all my senses, for some betrayal of that impending storm.

ANTONIA

So Avis wrote, waiting upon the Revolt of 1932, what some call the Second Revolt. It was to be brutal. The tortuous and distorted revolution of the next three centuries would compel the Revolt of 1953, the Revolt of 1981, the Revolt of 2016, and many more Revolts, all drowned in seas of blood, ere the world-movement of labor should come into its own.

AVIS

I am lonely. When I do not think of what is to come, I think of what has been and is no more— my Eagle, my Ernest, beating with tireless wings the void, soaring toward what was ever his sun, the flaming ideal of human freedom. I cannot sit idly by and await the great event that is his making, though he is not here to see. He devoted all the years of his manhood to it, and for it he gave his life. It is his handiwork. He made it.

ANTONIA

With all respect to Avis Everhard, it must be pointed out once more that Ernest was but one of many able leaders of the revolution.

AVIS

I shall try to write simply and to tell here how Ernest Everhard entered my life—how he grew until I became a part of him, and the tremendous changes he wrought in my life. In this way may you look at him through my eyes and learn him as I learned him—in all save the things too secret and sweet for me to tell.

SCENE 1 – CUNNINGHAM'S PARTY

(All stand. They are at a cocktail party.
BISHOP MOREHOUSE is in a discussion with
DR. HAMMERFELD. AVIS is talking with her
father, JOHN. ERNEST looks on.)

AVIS

It was in February, 1912, that I first met him,
when he appeared at a party in my father's house
in Berkeley.

JOHN

Avis, that dress looks lovely on you.

ANTONIA

John Cunningham, Avis Everhard's father, was
a physics professor at the State University at
Berkeley, California.

AVIS

Thank you father. But it must have been so
expensive!

JOHN

Nonsense. It's been a good year. And what else
would I spend it on?

AVIS

You never buy anything for yourself.

JOHN

I have all I need. Excuse me for a moment, I see Dr. Hammerfeld has arrived, I must say hello.

(JOHN walks over to HAMMERFELD. ERNEST approaches.)

ERNEST

Ernest Everhard.

AVIS

A pleasure to meet you, Mr. Everhard. Are you a prizefighter?

ERNEST

A prizefighter? Why would you think that?

ANTONIA

It was the custom of men in those days to compete for purses of money, in contests of hand-to-hand combat. When one was beaten into insensibility or killed, the survivor took the money.

AVIS

You have the look of one. And your hands.

ERNEST

What about them?

AVIS

I have not felt a hand so rough.

ERNEST

I am a working man.

DR. HAMMERFELD

A working man! How intriguing! Perhaps you could weigh in on a discussion I was having with Bishop Morehouse just now. We were wondering if the church does enough to aid the working class.

ERNEST

I am not schooled in such things.

JOHN

Go on. We respect the opinion of any man, if it is sincere.

ERNEST

All right then. If you truly want to hear my opinion, it is this: that you all know nothing, and worse than nothing, about the working class.

DR. HAMMERFELD

My dear boy, you may not realize it, but my doctorate is in sociology.

ERNEST

I'm sorry, but your sociology is both vicious and worthless.

DR. HAMMERFELD

What do you find so vicious and worthless, young man?

ERNEST

You are metaphysicians. You can prove anything by metaphysics; and having done so, every metaphysician can prove every other metaphysician wrong—to his own satisfaction. You are anarchists in the realm of thought. And you are mad cosmos-makers. Each of you dwells in a cosmos of his own making, created out of his own fancies and desires. You do not know the real world in which you live, and your thinking has no place in the real world except in so far as it is a phenomenon of mental aberration.

BISHOP MOREHOUSE

What would you have us be, instead?

ERNEST

Scientists. What good, what tangible good have metaphysicians wrought for mankind? They philosophized about the heart as the seat of the emotions, while the scientists were formulating the circulation of the blood. They declaimed about famine and pestilence as being scourges of God, while the scientists were building granaries and draining cities. They were describing the earth as the center of the universe, while the scientists were discovering America and probing space for the stars and the laws of the stars. In short, the metaphysicians have done nothing, absolutely nothing, for mankind. Step by step, before the advance of science, they have been driven back.

JOHN

Yet the thought of Aristotle ruled Europe for twelve centuries. And Aristotle was a metaphysician.

ERNEST

You refer to a very dark period in human history. A period wherein science was raped by the metaphysicians, wherein physics became a search for the Philosopher's Stone, wherein chemistry became alchemy, and astronomy became astrology. Sorry the domination of Aristotle's thought!

DR. HAMMERFELD

Who are you to say that sociology is not a science?

ERNEST

How can it be? You avow your knowledge of the working class, but it is clear you know nothing of it. You do not live in the same locality with the working class. You herd with the Capitalist class in another locality. And why not? It is the Capitalist class that pays you, that feeds you, that puts the very clothes on your backs that you are wearing tonight. And in return you preach to your employers the brands of metaphysics that are especially acceptable to them; and the especially acceptable brands are acceptable because they do not menace the established order of society.

BISHOP MOREHOUSE

I can assure you, we in the church are quite sincere in our desire to help.

JOHN

Indeed, I have listened to Bishop Morehouse here give many a sermon about the need for us to raise the living conditions of the less fortunate.

ERNEST

Oh, I am not challenging your sincerity. You are sincere. You preach what you believe. There lies your strength and your value—to the Capitalist class. But should you change your belief to something that menaces the established order, your preaching would be unacceptable to your employers, and you would be discharged.

JOHN

Excuse me if I ask, but how was it that you came to be invited to this party?

ERNEST

I wasn't. I saw the food and drink, and I was hungry. So I came in and I ate.

DR. HAMMERFELD

Then you are no more than a common thief!

ERNEST

You clearly have more food than you can eat yourselves. Would I be less a thief if I waited for your scraps at the garbage, so I could partake of them then?

AVIS

You introduced yourself to me as if you were a guest.

ERNEST

You are a lovely young woman. Why shouldn't I introduce myself?

JOHN

Eat the food, and welcome.

BISHOP MOREHOUSE

At least we can say in that way, we have helped the problem of the working class.

ERNEST

No, Bishop, you can say that in that way, I helped myself.

ANTONIA

The rest of Avis's account of that evening mostly concerns her romantic reactions to her future husband. She calls him:

AVIS

Unlike the men of my own class, so alien and so strong…

ANTONIA

And so forth. After that evening, Ernest became a frequent visitor to her father's house. To Avis' surprise, her father welcomed the young man. Her father was particularly taken by some of the songs Ernest shared, songs of the workers at the Sierra Mills and across America. Here is one that has survived to our day:

SONG: HARD TIMES AT THE MILL

COMPANY

Every mornin' at half-past four
You hear the cooks hop on the floor
It's hard times in the mill my love
Hard times in the mill

Every mornin' right at six
Don't that ol' bell make you sick
Hard times in the mill my love
Hard times in the mill

The pulley got hot, the belt jumped off
Knocked Mr. Guyan's derby off
It's hard times in the mill my love
Hard times in the mill

Section hand he thinks he's a man
He ain't got sense to pay off his hands
It's hard times in the mill my love
Hard times in the mill

My bobbin's all out, my end's all down
The doffer's in my alley an' I can't get around
It's hard times in the mill my love
Hard times in the mill

An' every night when I go home
A piece o' cornbread an' an ol' jawbone
It's hard times in the mill my love
Hard times in the mill

Ain't it enough to break your heart
Have to work all day, an' at night it's dark
It's hard times in the mill my love
Hard times in the mill

SCENE 2: AVIS AWAKENING

(AVIS steps forward with pamphlets
in hand.)

AVIS

Mr. Everhard, I have been reading these
pamphlets you have written. "Working Class
Philosophy." "Philosophy and Revolution."
What is their purpose?

ERNEST

They are propaganda, what else?

AVIS

Propaganda?

ERNEST

No revolution has ever been successful without
effective propaganda. The American Revolution.
The French Revolution. Christianity. We must
recognize that and use it to our advantage.
Those songs your father loves so much, they
are changing minds and changing hearts.
I hope my pamphlets can do the same.

AVIS

Then I have a quarrel with you. You foment class
hatred. I consider it wrong and criminal to appeal
to all that is narrow and brutal in the working class.

Class hatred is anti-social, and, it seems to me, anti-Socialistic.

ERNEST

But there is no mention of class hatred.

AVIS

In your pamphlets, you call it "class struggle."

ERNEST

That is a different thing. Class struggle is a law of social development. We are not responsible for it. We do not make the class struggle. We merely explain it, as Newton explained gravitation. We explain the nature of the conflict of interest that produces the class struggle. The conflict of interest between labor and capital.

AVIS

But why should there be a conflict of interest?

ERNEST

Indeed, why should there be? Perhaps it is because we are so made. Would you agree that the average man is selfish?

AVIS

Perhaps. But he ought not to be.

ERNEST

He ought not to be selfish, but he will continue
to be selfish as long as he lives in a social system
that is based on pig-ethics.

AVIS

Pig-ethics?

ERNEST

Laissez-faire, the let-alone policy of each for
himself and devil take the hindmost. The
wild Indian is not so brutal and savage
as the Capitalist class.

AVIS

You do not know us. We are not brutal and
savage.

ERNEST

Prove it.

AVIS

How can I prove it to you?

ERNEST

Prove it to yourself.

AVIS

I know it.

ERNEST

I understand you have money, or your father has, which is the same thing, invested in Sierra Mills.

AVIS

What has that to do with anything?

ERNEST

Nothing much. Except that the gown you wear is stained with blood. The food you eat is a bloody stew. The blood of little children and of strong men is dripping from your very roof-beams. I can close my eyes, now, and hear it drip, drop, drip, drop, all about me.

(AVIS looks at him in horror.)

AVIS

One needs money to live! Is not your money stained with blood? Where does it come from?

ERNEST

Mine came from labor at first, and then from my colleagues, the Socialists. We support each other, when in need, and we don't need much. I will introduce you to them one day soon I think.

(JACKSON stands and lifts a chair onto his back.)

JACKSON

It was then that a man, passing along the sidewalk, stopped and looked in at them. He was poorly dressed, and on his back was a great load of rattan and bamboo stands, chairs, and screens. He looked at the house as if debating whether or not he should come in and try to sell some of his wares.

ERNEST

That man's name is Jackson.

AVIS

With that strong body of his he should be at work, and not peddling.

(JACKSON has slipped an arm into his shirt, to give himself the appearance of a one-armed man. ERNEST continues, in a gentle tone.)

ERNEST

Notice the sleeve of his left arm. It was some of the blood from that arm that I heard dripping from your roof-beams. He lost his arm in the Sierra Mills, and like a broken-down horse you turned him out on the highway to die. When I say "you," I mean the superintendent and the officials that you and the other stockholders pay to manage the mills for you. It was an accident.

It was caused by his trying to save the company a few dollars. The toothed drum of the picker caught his arm. He might have let the small flint that he saw in the teeth go through. It would have smashed out a double row of spikes. But he reached for the flint, and his arm was picked and clawed to shreds from the finger tips to the shoulder. It was at night. The mills were working overtime. They paid a fat dividend that quarter. Jackson had been working many hours, and his muscles had lost their resiliency and snap. They made his movements a bit slow. That was why the machine caught him.

AVIS

And what did the company do for him?

ERNEST

Nothing. Oh, yes, they did do something. They successfully fought the damage suit he brought when he came out of hospital. The company employs very efficient lawyers, you know.

AVIS

You have not told the whole story. Or else you do not know the whole story. Maybe the man was insolent.

ERNEST

Insolent! Great God! Insolent! And with his
arm chewed off! Nevertheless he was a meek
and lowly servant, and there is no record of his
having been insolent.

AVIS

But the courts. The case would not have been
decided against him had there been no more to
the affair than you have mentioned.

ERNEST

Colonel Ingram is leading counsel for the
company. He is a shrewd lawyer. I tell you what
you do, Miss Cunningham. You investigate
Jackson's case.

AVIS

I intend to.

ERNEST

I'll tell you where to find him. But I tremble for
you when I think of all you are to prove by
Jackson's arm.

SCENE 3: JACKSON

(ERNEST sits. AVIS approaches JACKSON,
who slowly and laboriously rids himself of
his chair.)

ANTONIA

It is hard for us to imagine the dwelling of a man
such as Jackson today. He lived out near the
marsh. Pools of stagnant water stood around his
house, their surfaces covered with a green and
putrid-looking scum, while the stench that arose
from them was intolerable. For this privilege he
paid rent, enormous rent, to his landlords.

JACKSON

They might a-given me a job as a watchman,
anyway.

AVIS

How did you happen to get your arm caught in
the machine?

JACKSON

I don't know. It just happened.

AVIS

Carelessness?

JACKSON

No. I ain't for callin' it that. I was workin' overtime, an' I guess I was tired out some. I worked seventeen years in them mills, an' I've took notice that most of the accidents happens just before whistle-blow.

ANTONIA

The laborers of the time were called to work and dismissed by savage, screaming, nerve-racking steam-whistles.

JACKSON

I'm willin' to bet that more accidents happens in the hour before whistle-blow than in all the rest of the day. A man ain't so quick after workin' steady for hours. I've seen too many of 'em cut up an' gouged an' chawed not to know.

AVIS

Many of them?

JACKSON

Hundreds an' hundreds, an' children too.

AVIS

Did you violate some sort of safety rule?

JACKSON

No, ma'am. I chucked off the belt with my right hand, an' made a reach for the flint with my left. I didn't stop to see if the belt was off. I thought my right hand had done it—only it didn't. I reached quick, and the belt wasn't all the way off. And then my arm was chawed off.

AVIS

It must have been painful.

JACKSON

The crunchin' of the bones wasn't nice.

AVIS

And your lawsuit?

JACKSON

I don't rightfully know. Someone said somethin' that wasn't what it ought to have been, I guess. So now I peddle. And my eldest, he works in the mill.

AVIS

But aren't you afraid he might have an accident?

JACKSON

I don't see that we have much choice, if we
want to eat. They might a-given me a job as
watchman, anyway.

ANTONIA

In those days, enormous numbers of men were
employed as watchmen to protect property.
Thievery was incredibly prevalent. The lords
of society stole legally or else legalized their
stealing, while the poorer classes stole illegally.
Nothing was safe unless guarded.

SCENE 4: CHURCH RECEPTION

AVIS

Jackson marked just the beginning of my journey. Through him, I met another man whose leg had been destroyed when a machine had fallen on it. Through him, the widow of a man who had been struck in the head. Through her, three others. None had been compensated by the mill. Some had resorted to the law, and some, seeing it as a futile gesture, had not bothered. Colonel Ingram, the company lawyer, had a reputation for never losing a case. A few days after I had met Jackson, I saw Colonel Ingram at a church reception, and decided to confront him.

> (INGRAM stands, smiles at AVIS in a friendly, open way.)

INGRAM

My dear, what can it be that you need to speak about, with such urgency?

AVIS

It is about a man name Jackson. A worker, injured at the mill. Do you know him?

> (INGRAM looks away, his smile replaced by something grimmer.)

INGRAM

I do.

AVIS

And you were the lawyer that represented the Mill against him?

INGRAM

I was.

AVIS

Do you think he should have received damages?

INGRAM

I think his case was a tragedy.

AVIS

Yes, but do you think he received what he deserved?

INGRAM

I think he deserves as much as can be given to him. But that has nothing to do with the law.

AVIS

Do you think you had moral right on your side?

INGRAM

Legal right.

AVIS

By which you mean, might?

INGRAM

Some call it that.

AVIS

Then how are we supposed to get justice by means of the law?

INGRAM

Justice is the only thing the law provides. That is the paradox.

AVIS

Is this your personal feeling?

INGRAM

I am speaking as one whose profession is the law.

AVIS

But what are your personal feelings, your feelings as a spiritual man?

INGRAM

I'm so sorry, my dear, you wish me to speak against my employers. You must understand, I cannot. If you will excuse me.

(INGRAM crosses and sits.)

AVIS

At that same function, I spotted Mrs. Wickson, the wife of one of the mill owners. She had a reputation for contributing to charity, or at least I had heard her speak of doing so on many occasions. So I decided to appeal to her charitable side.

ANTONIA

Mrs. Wickson was what was called at the time a "society woman." In the minds of the wealthy, the only people who participated in society were the idle rich, not the common laborers.

(MRS. WICKSON stands, drink in hand.)

AVIS

Mrs. Wickson, is there any way you can help this poor man?

MRS. WICKSON

Avis, you must understand. To give him money would be to reward him for his carelessness.

AVIS

But his situation is desperate. Even if he was careless in his exhaustion, doesn't the mill have an obligation to take care of its workers?

MRS. WICKSON

Indeed we do. And it is for that very reason that I refuse. Think, by paying him, I would tempt others to hurt themselves similarly.

AVIS

Who would voluntarily put himself through that horror?

MRS. WICKSON

You are young and sheltered, Avis, and I do not think you understand the mind of the working class.

(MRS. WICKSON walks away. AVIS is back with ERNEST, who stands.)

SCENE 5: MARRIAGE PROPOSAL

AVIS

That evening, Ernest came to call again. He found me in a dismal mood.

ERNEST

So, did you speak with Jackson?

AVIS

I did.

ERNEST

And?

AVIS

I—I think some of his blood is dripping from our roof-beams.

ERNEST

Of course, if Jackson and his fellows were treated mercifully, the dividends that your father receives would not be as large.

AVIS

I shall never be able to take pleasure in pretty gowns again.

ERNEST

When we are married, you will delight in other things.

AVIS

Are we to be married?

ERNEST

Of course. I thought that was assumed.

AVIS

Ernest, you are so articulate when you speak about the plight of the working class, indeed I can hardly pause you when it comes to politics. But when it comes to love, you have not said a word.

ERNEST

Haven't you assumed it is our fate, as well?

AVIS

Perhaps. But you have not so much as kissed me.

(ERNEST kisses her.)

ERNEST

There. We are engaged.

AVIS

It was a nice kiss. Do you have a priest hidden behind the door to finish the matter?

ERNEST

Must we have a priest?

AVIS

We must have the Bishop Morehouse. But why are we discussing this, no date has been set.

ERNEST

What date would you prefer?

AVIS

We should talk to my father about it first.

ERNEST

Very well. Where is he?

AVIS

Now?

ERNEST

Why not?

AVIS

He is at a meeting of the Philomath's Club. They are assembling at Bishop Morehouse's church tonight.

ERNEST

Very well, let's join him.

AVIS

Ernest, we haven't been invited.

ERNEST

If I waited to be invited, I would never be admitted anywhere. And we should never have met. Besides, doesn't a church have the obligation to welcome all comers?

AVIS

I suppose that's true.

ERNEST

Then let us go to see your father.

SCENE 6: THE PHILOMATH'S CLUB

ANTONIA

Let me say a word about the Philomath's Club. In the early twentieth century, it was common for men to belong to clubs. Some were created for a specific purpose, to join the like minded. Some existed merely for the camaraderie. The Philomath's Club was a mixture of the two. It was created to be a forum in which men discussed great ideas. Over time, like many such clubs, it became a bastion for the elite, a place barred to women and the working class so that the men who ruled could sustain their ruling status. This new purpose was never stated explicitly, but it became clear as the membership grew to include prominent members of the Oligarchy, including Mr. Wickson, of Sierra Mills. Yet a vestige of its original purpose remained.

BISHOP MOREHOUSE

Ernest, how good of you to come! I am most pleased to see you.

ERNEST

Are you?

BISHOP MOREHOUSE

Of course. In fact, as you will see, my whole address this evening has been partly inspired by our recent discussions.

WICKSON

Who is this man?

JOHN

His name is Ernest Everhard. We made his acquaintance recently, and since then he and my daughter have become quite close. I must say, I am surprised to see you both here.

WICKSON

Everhard… I have heard that name before…

JOHN

Mr. Everhard, if I might introduce Mr. Wickson.

ERNEST

We have met.

WICKSON

I think so too. But where?

ERNEST

I was one your workers, at the mill.

WICKSON

At my mill!

AVIS

Ernest, you never told me that you worked at the mill yourself.

ERNEST

You knew I was a working man. Yes, I worked at the mill. Until I was fired for insubordination.

WICKSON

I see. You were one of those union organizers.

ERNEST

I stood up for a man named Jackson, who had been injured through no fault of his own. And for that, I lost my job.

WICKSON

Yes, now I remember. You had a knack for turning a hard day's work into exploitation. You and your Iron Heel. I remember.

AVIS

Your Iron Heel?

ERNEST

My metaphor for the machinery of the Oligarchy, that grinds down anything beneath it.

WICKSON

Who let this man in here? I demand that he be removed.

BISHOP MOREHOUSE

This is a church, Mr. Wickson. All who wish to enter must be welcomed.

AVIS

Besides which, he is my fiancé.

JOHN

Your fiancé?

AVIS

I'm sorry Father, I didn't mean to tell you like this.

JOHN

When did this happen?

AVIS

Just now.

ERNEST

It happened the moment we met, sir. We just put it into words today.

(WICKSON laughs.)

WICKSON

Do you truly expect your father to agree to this arrangement? He is not only a distinguished professor, but he is one of the shareholders in our mill, as well. If my daughter came home to tell me she was marrying a laborer, or rather a former laborer, now unemployed, I assure you I would not let her out of my sight again. Do you even have a penny to your name?

ERNEST

I have more than money, I have my fellow Socialists who sustain me. They give to me when I am in need, as I have given to them in the past.

WICKSON

In other words, you are a beggar.

JOHN

I have not known him long, Mr. Wickson, but he has struck me as an honorable man, who cares for my daughter quite honestly. That is all I would ask from him.

WICKSON

He will drag your daughter with him through the muck.

BISHOP MOREHOUSE

Gentlemen, please. We have gathered here
to take part in an exploration of philosophy,
knowledge, and humanity. I have a story I think is
of great importance, and perhaps, when you hear
it, this dispute may fade away.

WICKSON

We cannot all be Jesus, Bishop.

BISHOP MOREHOUSE

Of course not, Mr. Wickson. In fact, until recently,
I had not realized how far I myself had strayed
from his teachings. But now my eyes have opened.
A few nights ago I was in my brougham, driving
through the streets. I looked through the carriage
windows, and saw a woman peddling herself. At
first I covered my eyes with my hands to shut out
the awful sight, and then, in the darkness, the
question came to me: What is to be done? What
is to be done? Then the question came to me in
another way: What would the Master do? And
a great light seemed to fill the place, and I saw
my duty sun-clear, as Saul saw his on the way to
Damascus.

(Breaks character for a second.)

Antonia, would you mind playing the prostitute?
I'm going to enact their encounter.

ANTONIA

Oh! Of course…does she have lines?

BISHOP MOREHOUSE

You can make up a few, if you like.

ANTONIA

I can give it a try. I haven't acted since I performed in a play at my Communal Education Center, when I was just a girl.

BISHOP MOREHOUSE

Would you like to get in the carriage with me?

ANTONIA

I would imagine she might say…why not, I have never sold my sexual services to a Bishop before. Considering my current state of poverty, my priority is monetary acquisition.

BISHOP MOREHOUSE

I assure you, I see you as a sister, nothing more. But I can offer you some food and some money if you need it. Or a place to stay if you need one. Where do you live?

ANTONIA

A woman such as this would typically live in a crowded tenement apartment, if she had any permanent home at all. Often, her whoremonger would take her rent out of her wages, creating a state of permanent indebtedness.'

BISHOP MOREHOUSE

Then by all means, you must stay with me. Hearing you speak of your circumstances, I realize that my house must seem to you a mansion. No, a palace. I never knew what palaces were good for. I had thought they were to live in. But now I know. They are for you and your sisters, a safe haven made to show honor to those who have fallen by the wayside.

ANTONIA

I imagine that she might be afraid she would be made to feel wicked for her occupation.

BISHOP MOREHOUSE

I am not fit to tell you anything about morality. I have lived with shame and hypocrisy too long. But to those who believe in Jesus and his gospel there can be no other relation between man and man than the relation of affection. Love alone is stronger than sin—stronger than death. It is my duty to help you in any way I can.

(Turns to assembly.)

And I say to you all, that you share this duty to do what I have done and am doing. Let each one of you who is prosperous take into his house some thief and treat him as his brother, some unfortunate and treat her as his sister, and San Francisco will need no police force and no magistrates; the prisons will be turned into hospitals, and the criminal will disappear with his crime. Do not harden your hearts. Do not close your ears to the voices that are crying in the land—the voices of pain and sorrow that you refuse to hear but that some day will be heard. And so I say—

WICKSON

I did not come here to be made to feel small!

BISHOP MOREHOUSE

I assure you, that was not my intention.

WICKSON

First, you allow this revolutionist to attend our meeting. Then you preach at me in his language. I am amazed and disgusted. What you do not seem to realize is that we are on the edge of a war, a war between us and men like this revolutionist here.

BISHOP MOREHOUSE

I hardly think that is the case.

WICKSON

Then you are a blind fool. There are a million and a half revolutionists in the United States, and they are ready to try to take everything we hold dear. That is a fact. Go ahead, ask this man here if that isn't true. You do not know him, but I do. He is one of the worst of them, one of their leaders.

ERNEST

You are wrong. You underestimate us. The army is not a million and a half strong, it is twenty-five million strong. We are going to take your governments, your palaces, and all your purpled ease away from you, and in that day you shall work for your bread even as the peasant in the field or the starved and runty clerk in your metropolises. Why do you think the managers of society did not make public the census figures of 1910? I will answer for you: they were afraid to admit how many millions of people in the United States today live in abject poverty, without food, without adequate shelter. The revolution is gathering. We want in our hands the reins of power and the destiny of mankind. Here are our hands. They are strong hands!

WICKSON

When you reach out your vaunted strong hands for our palaces and purpled ease, we will show you what strength is. In roar of shell and shrapnel and in whine of machine-guns will our answer be couched. We will grind you revolutionists down under our heel, and we shall walk upon your faces. The world is ours, we are its lords, and ours it shall remain. As for the host of labor, it has been in the dirt since history began, if I read history aright. And in the dirt it shall remain so long as I and mine and those that come after us have the power. There is the word. It is the king of words—Power. Not God, not Mammon, but Power. Pour it over your tongue till it tingles with it. Power.

ERNEST

I agree with you. I agree with all that you have said. Power will be the arbiter, as it always has been the arbiter. It is a struggle of classes. Just as your class dragged down the old feudal nobility, so shall it be dragged down by my class, the working class. If you will read your biology and your sociology as clearly as you do your history, you will see that this end I have described is inevitable. It does not matter whether it is in one year, ten, or a thousand—your class shall be dragged down. And it shall be done by power. We of the labor hosts have conned that word over till our minds are all a-tingle with it. Power. It is a kingly word.

ACTOR

I'm sorry, Antonia, I know we discussed this in rehearsal, but this does feel a little extreme.

It is great fun to play a character as wicked as
Wickson, of course, but was he so blatant in what
he said? "We will grind you under our heel," and
all that?

ANTONIA

He knew his power as a minor oligarch was
dependent on his oppression of the working
class, so of course.

ACTOR

But even if that was how he felt, would he have
stated it like that?

ANTONIA

I am certain of it. Shall we continue?

SCENE 7: THE UNIVERSITY

AVIS

So ended the night with the Philomaths. It was
to be a foreshadowing of worse, much worse
to come. Disaster approached on padded feet.
Two days after that evening, it was reported that
Bishop Morehouse had gone away on a vacation
to recover from the effects of overwork. It was
whispered that his work had led to nervous
collapse, or maybe insanity, though I had seen no
signs of it. Then my father received news from his
university that set him into a fury.

JOHN

I had a luncheon with the university president. I
was sent for.

ERNEST

And you were reprimanded. For your association
with me.

JOHN

How did you guess?

ERNEST

It is nothing to what will come.

JOHN

There was gossip about Avis being seen in public
with so notorious a character as you, and he
said it was not in keeping with university tone
and dignity. Not that he personally objected—
oh, no; but that there was talk and that I would
understand. I made it pretty awkward for him,
and he could only go on repeating himself
and telling me how much he honored me as a
scientist. It wasn't an agreeable task for him.
I could see he didn't like it.

ERNEST

He was not a free agent. The leg-bar is not always
worn graciously.

ANTONIA

African slaves were so manacled; also criminals. It
was not until the coming of our modern Socialist
society that the leg-bar passed out of use.

JOHN

He offered me a two years' vacation, on full pay,
in Europe, for recreation and research. Of course
I couldn't accept it under the circumstances.

ERNEST

There is more behind this than a mere university
ideal. Somebody has put pressure on him.

JOHN

Do you think so?

ERNEST

You heard Wickson just the other day. There is a shadow of something colossal and menacing that even now is beginning to fall across the land. Call it the shadow of an Oligarchy, if you will. But what I wanted to say was this: You are in a perilous position—a peril that my own fear enhances because I am not able even to measure it. Take my advice and accept the vacation.

JOHN

They can't hurt me. I am independent. I have not been a professor for the sake of my salary. I can get along very comfortably on my own income, and the salary is all they can take away from me.

ERNEST

If all that I fear be so, your private income, your principal itself, can be taken from you just as easily as your salary.

JOHN

It would be cowardly.

ERNEST

I urge you, you do not know them as I do. They will do everything they can to destroy you.

JOHN

You have sung me your songs. I have read your propaganda. So now you see you have persuaded me. Let them take what they might.

AVIS

Afterwards, I asked Ernest why he advised my father to quit, if he himself was such an unwavering supporter of the revolution.

ERNEST

Because I love you and, like Ruth of old, thy people are my people.

(They kiss.)

SCENE 8: THE BLACK HUNDREDS

AVIS

From that moment on, events began to fall about us thick and fast. Capitalism collapsed from its own weight, and the years of prosperity needed to be paid for. Suddenly, all markets were glutted; all markets were falling; and amidst the general crumble of prices the price of labor crumbled fastest of all.

> (ACTORS pick up signs. In the background, they chant "Strike!")

Labor was striking here, there, and everywhere; and where it was not striking, it was being turned out by the Capitalists. The papers were filled with tales of violence and blood. And through it all the Black Hundreds played their part.

ANTONIA

The Black Hundreds were the secret agents of the Oligarchy, who disguised themselves as workers and used violence in order to destroy the reputation of the working class. They are memorialized in this song:

SONG: WHICH SIDE ARE YOU ON?

COMPANY

A crowd of striking workers
Then suddenly a shot
I know each face around me
But this one I do not

He shouts for revolution
He turns the hall to red
And when the shooting ceases
One hundred lay there dead

Chorus
Which side are you on, friend?
Which side are you on?
Tell me, which side are you on, friend?
Which side are you on?

They waited for the violence
They knew that it would come
A crowd of striking workers
Refusing to succumb

But when we would not fire
An agent they did send
The seed of our destruction
Disguised as if a friend

Which side are you on, friend?
Which side are you on?
Tell me, which side are you on, friend?
Which side are you on?

They call themselves Black Hundreds
Within our midst they steal
But do not doubt they're serving
Their boss, the Iron Heel

Which side are you on, friend?
Which side are you on?
Tell me, which side are you on, friend?
Which side are you on?

(Sound of gunfire.)

AVIS

It was a massacre. Never had labor received such an all-around beating. The great captains of industry, the oligarchs, had for the first time thrown their full weight into the breach. Labor was bloody and sullen, but crushed. Yet its defeat did not put an end to the hard times. The banks, themselves constituting one of the most important forces of the Oligarchy, continued to call in credits. The Wall Street group turned the stock market into a maelstrom where the values of all the stock crumbled away almost to nothingness.

ANTONIA

Wall Street was a street in ancient New York, where the irrational organization of society permitted underhanded manipulation of all the wealth in the country.

AVIS

As the stocks plummeted, the fortunes of the middle class plummeted as well. The oligarchs alone knew how to reap the whirlwind and make a profit out of it. And such profits! Colossal profits! They swiftly plundered the wrecks that floated about them, as if they had anticipated the storm all along. Even Ernest was astounded at the quickness.

ERNEST

It's no use. We are beaten. The Iron Heel is triumphant. Wickson was right. We shall be robbed of our few remaining liberties; the Iron Heel will walk upon our faces; nothing remains but a bloody revolution of the working class. Of course we will win, but I shudder to think of it.

AVIS

Ernest took me to a meeting with his fellow Socialists. They insisted that victory could be gained through the elections.

SCENE 9: THE SOCIALISTS, PART 1

SOCIALIST 1

You must run for Congress, Ernest. The majority is with us. If enough people sympathetic with our cause run for Congress, we can turn the tide.

ERNEST

And when they take me out of Congress, and put me against a wall, and blow my brains out— what then?

SOCIALISTS

Then we rise in might!

ERNEST

Then you'll welter in your gore. I've heard that same song sung by the middle class. Where now is their might?

SOCIALIST 2

It is either you or Wickson.

ERNEST

Wickson?

SOCIALIST 3

Didn't you hear? He announced his candidacy
just yesterday.

ERNEST

Of course. It is their way of operation, control
the government and thereby control the worker.
But Wickson…he is the worst, the very worst of
them. Very well. I fear it is a helpless cause, but
I will run.

AVIS

What will that mean for you, Ernest? What will
that mean for us?

ERNEST

It means we must marry immediately, before the
tide of events pulls us apart.

AVIS

I still insisted that I wanted Bishop Morehouse
to perform the ceremony, and no other. Ernest
seemed quietly doubtful, but did not try to stop
me from visiting the Bishop.

SCENE 10: THE DISSOLUTION OF THE BISHOP

(The BISHOP enters, clutching a bag
of potatoes.)

BISHOP MOREHOUSE

I have put my home on the market.

AVIS

But it is so beautiful. And what of the woman you
were housing here?

BISHOP MOREHOUSE

Yes, it is true. But there are so many…I could do
so much more, much more than I am doing…．
The house…the paintings…the library…I could
be using that money to feed someone.

AVIS

You must not ruin yourself.

BISHOP MOREHOUSE

The potatoes…they are precious…

AVIS

Is that a bag of them I see?

BISHOP MOREHOUSE

There is an old woman. I must take it to her at once. She is suffering from want of it. I must go at once. You understand. Then I will return. I promise you.

AVIS

But Bishop, I have come to talk to you about my marriage—

BISHOP MOREHOUSE

An old German woman. Sixty-four. Her hands are misshapen from rheumatism, but all she does is sew, from morning till night. Six cents per pair of trousers, each trouser takes two hours. Her only daughter died when a boiler exploded in the factory. No one to take care of her but me.

AVIS

I will go with you.

BISHOP MOREHOUSE

It is your Ernest who is responsible for this change in me.

AVIS

It is too much for you to bear.

BISHOP MOREHOUSE

I am grateful. I have him to thank for showing me my path. And I am very happy, only... Only the persecution. I harm no one. Why will they not let me alone? But it is not that. It is the nature of the persecution. I shouldn't mind if they cut my flesh with stripes, or burned me at the stake, or crucified me head-downward. But it is the asylum that frightens me. Think of it! Of me—in an asylum for the insane! It is revolting. I saw some of the cases at the sanitarium. They were violent. My blood chills when I think of it. And to be imprisoned for the rest of my life amid scenes of screaming madness! No! no! Not that! Not that!

(He pauses, shaking.)

AVIS

I will not let them. Ernest will not let them.

BISHOP MOREHOUSE

Forgive me. It is my wretched nerves. And if the Master's work leads there, so be it. Who am I to complain? Soon my house will be sold. All my other possessions. I must do it secretly, else they will take everything away from me. I often marvel these days at the immense quantity of potatoes two or three hundred thousand dollars will buy, or bread, or meat, or coal and kindling.

AVIS

Ernest is entering politics. I know things have gotten bad, but he is working to change it for the better. And we are to be married soon. That is what I have come to tell you. You must officiate at our wedding.

BISHOP MOREHOUSE

You will need to find someone else. I cannot be seen in public, not now. They will put me in a madhouse. But tell your young man that I have at last found my work in the world. It is the Master's work. You caught me feeding his lambs. And of course you will both keep my secret.

SCENE 11: ERNEST REFUSES

AVIS

I ran to Ernest, to beg him to talk the Bishop out of his plans to impoverish himself. But Ernest refused.

ERNEST

No matter how small the good, nevertheless his little inadequate wail will be productive of some good in the revolution, and every little bit counts.

AVIS

Perhaps the Church can protect him.

ERNEST

Christ told the rich young man to sell all he had. The Bishop has decided to obey Christ's injunction, and it will get him locked up in a madhouse. Times have changed since Christ's day. A rich man today who gives all he has to the poor is crazy. There is no discussion. Society has spoken.

AVIS

But the Church—

ERNEST

He has left the Church already. The Church feeds at the same trough as the Oligarchy, and together they will be his ruin.

AVIS

Then why will you not try to dissuade him? When you just advised my father to take the easier path and quit the university, the other day?

ERNEST

I cannot protect the world from the ravages of the revolution. I have chosen you, and I have chosen your father, and I am selfish. Yes, I am selfish. I know what is to come, and I have chosen to protect my family, but I cannot protect the world.

AVIS

Is that why? Or is it because you despise the Church?

ERNEST

I have told you, your Bishop has left the Church. The more's the pity for him.

AVIS

Isn't his downfall, the very reason that he is persecuted, because he listened to you and your Socialist ideas?

ERNEST

If he had truly listened to me, he would be taking up arms. The revolution cannot be won by good deeds alone.

AVIS

He is not a violent man.

ERNEST

Neither am I. But I understand the necessity.

AVIS

Perhaps, if the revolution had leaders like the Bishop, violence wouldn't be as necessary.

ERNEST

The Bishop is not a leader.

AVIS

Then a man like him.

ERNEST

Such men are fantasies, I'm afraid. I understand why you would long for them. But they are fantasies.

ACTOR

Surely that's not true. I'm sorry to interrupt again, Antonia, but I know there are leaders who believe in peace.

ANTONIA

Now yes. But then…we needed the hundreds of years of revolution in order to arrive here, today. That is a scientific fact.

AVIS

A week later we were married, by a man I had never seen before in my life and never would see after. Only my father attended.

(JOHN hands AVIS an envelope.)

JOHN

Take this gift. Towards the cause. I have sold the house. My money disappeared along with the stocks, just like everyone else. No matter, I am happy for you, and for myself. I have my freedom. My beliefs are my own, no man can change that.

SCENE 12: THE SOCIALISTS, PART 2

AVIS

A few days after that I read that the Bishop had been committed to the Napa Asylum. In vain we tried to see him. Later we learned he had been transferred to Stockton, to Agnews, and then all the way off to Chicago. After that, we heard no more. In the meantime, events conspired in the Socialist's favor for once.

SOCIALIST 1

Hearst has gone bankrupt!

ANTONIA

William Randolph Hearst was a young California millionaire who became the most powerful newspaper owner in the country. His newspapers were published in all the large cities, and they appealed to the perishing middle class and to the proletariat. So large was his following that he managed to take possession of the empty shell of the old Democratic Party. He occupied an anomalous position, preaching an emasculated Socialism combined with a nondescript sort of petty bourgeois Capitalism. It was oil and water, and there was no hope for him, though for a short period he was a source of serious apprehension to the Plutocrats.

ERNEST

Bankrupt? How?

SOCIALIST 1

By fiat of the Plutocrats! They have colluded to
stop advertising in his papers and have driven
him out of business. The Democrats do not
know how to run a party without the crutch
of his millions.

SOCIALIST 2

The perfect opening!

SOCIALIST 1

We know how to run a campaign without
depending on Hearst. And what better time
than now, when the workers are crying for an
authentic voice? Your voice.

ERNEST

Our voice.

SOCIALIST 2

It is the end of Capitalism.

ERNEST

It is the end of the Democratic Party, perhaps.
But machinery of Capitalism will not be broken
so easily. We must spread our propaganda. The
time for newspapers is over. It will take an army
of us, mouth to mouth.

SOCIALIST 1

We have an army.

ERNEST

And we must organize a public debate.

SOCIALIST 3

Wickson will never agree to it.

ERNEST

We must give him no choice. We must make the people demand it.

SOCIALIST 3

Do you think it's possible?

ERNEST

If we are to have any chance of winning, we must be heard. It is time to call for a General Strike. We will refuse to work in their factories until they agree to include us in the next public debate. We have the people, and the will, now more than ever, now that the workers have seen the bloodthirsty power of the Oligarchs. Spread the word. No work until the Socialist Workers Party is allowed a voice!

SOCIALIST 2

We will prevail! I can feel it.

ERNEST

I wish I could believe it. But I think blood, much
more blood will be shed before we can crawl out
from under the Iron Heel.

AVIS

It happened much as Ernest projected—at first.
The Socialists demanded to be included in the
next debate. The Democrats and Republicans
resisted. A General Strike was threatened, but
support for it was uncertain. It seemed for a
while, that perhaps the Oligarchy would prevail.
Then the Honolulu Affair changed everything.

ANTONIA

In 1912, after years of tension about the world
market, a German fleet attacked Honolulu,
sinking three ships and bombarding the city.
The next day, war was declared between America
and Germany. Within an hour, the call for a
General Strike was finally heeded, not only by the
American Socialists, but by the German Socialists
as well. Without the support of the workers, the
machinery of war quickly ground to a halt.

AVIS

The women proved to be the strongest
promoters of the strike. They set their faces
against the war. They did not want their men
to go forth to die. Then, also, the idea of the
General Strike caught the mood of the people.

It struck their sense of humor. The idea was infectious. The children struck in all the schools, and such teachers as came, went home again from deserted classrooms. The general strike took the form of a great national picnic. For a week, it was as if the world of the Oligarchy had ceased to exist. And for once, Ernest was optimistic.

ERNEST

Perhaps I was wrong. Perhaps we won't need bloodshed after all.

SOCIALIST 1

They've agreed to our terms. They will allow you to participate in the next debate. And not only you. The Socialist Workers Party candidates have been invited to take part in debates across the country.

ERNEST

One last ditch effort to confront us and turn the world back towards war, no doubt.

SOCIALIST 1

They underestimate you.

ERNEST

No, they underestimate the workers. They will not be swayed by rhetoric and fear-mongering. So I will be debating Wickson directly?

SOCIALIST 1

The Democrat will be there too, of course.
James Roberts.

ERNEST

A weak man and a weaker candidate. He may call
himself a Democrat, but he has spent his life as
part of the Oligarchy.

AVIS

Be careful, Ernest.

ERNEST

Of what?

AVIS

I don't know. Didn't you tell me that the
Oligarchy will not die so easily?

ERNEST

Of course not. This is just one of a number of
blows. But the General Strike has left them
reeling. They never anticipated our power.

(The SOCIALISTS hand out flyers as they sing.)

SONG: POWER IN A UNION

COMPANY

There is pow'r there is pow'r in a band
of working folk
When they stand hand in hand,
That's a pow'r, that's a pow'r
That must rule in every land—
One Industrial Union Grand.

Would you have freedom from wage slavery
Then join in the Grand Industrial Band;
Would you from mis'ry and hunger be free,
Then come, do your share, lend a hand.

There is pow'r there is pow'r in a band
of working folk,
When they stand hand in hand,
That's a pow'r, that's a pow'r
That must rule in every land—
One Industrial Union Grand.

Would you fight battles in far Germany
To fill up the purses of the Oligarchy
Vote for the Socialist Workers Party
We can change the world, you and me

There is pow'r there is pow'r in a band
of working folk,
When they stand hand in hand,
That's a pow'r, that's a pow'r
That must rule in every land—
One Industrial Union Grand.

Come, all ye workers, from every land,
Come, join in the Grand Industrial Band;
Then we our share of this earth shall demand.
Come on! Do your share, lend a hand.

There is pow'r there is pow'r in a band
of working folk,
When they stand hand in hand,
That's a pow'r, that's a pow'r
That must rule in every land—
One Industrial Union Grand.

SCENE 13: THE DEBATE

(ANTONIA holds up a poster, announcing
the debate.)

ANTONIA

I have located an old poster, announcing
the debate, in the National Archives. This is a
facsimile of it. It is here that I must remind you
that, although for Avis of course her husband
was at the center of this story, he was but one
of many Socialist leaders of the time. Across the
United States, Socialist leaders were, for the first
time ever, put on equal footing as the two major
parties. And the debates were coordinated,
over twenty of them, all on the same date. April
20, 1912. Do you remember hearing that date
in school? Maybe so. Now you will learn the
true significance of that day to those who were
unlucky enough to be part of history.

(ERNEST stands on a soapbox.)

ERNEST

Your eyes have been opened. You have witnessed
the might of our combined will. Together, we
have ended a war before it even began. Who
wanted that war? The Plutocracy. Who controls
the government today? The proletariat with its
twenty millions? No. Does the middle class, with
its eight million? No more than the proletariat.

Who, then, controls the government? The Plutocracy, a mere quarter million, the top nine-tenths of one percent in wealth. There is no Democratic Party. There is no Republican Party. There are only lick-spittlers and panderers, creatures of that top nine-tenths. But we have proven that we can rise up and claim what is rightfully ours. Vote for Wickson and you vote for a continuation of the Oligarchy. Vote for Roberts and you will get the same, he too is a servant of the machine. Vote for me and you vote for yourselves. I will not be so arrogant as to believe that I am more important than any one of you. Your eyes have been opened at last, do not let them close.

(WICKSON and WASHINGTON step up.)

WICKSON

I come with good news. The General Strike is over. Not because of Everhard and his motley crew of revolutionaries, extremists whose only interest is bringing anarchy to our great land. But because of reasonable men, reasonable men like myself and Mr. Washington here. Mr. Washington is the head of the union that represents the iron and steel workers that I employ. Why is he here? Because together, we have forged an agreement, an agreement that brings higher pay and shortened hours. I have been working on similar deals such as with the railway workers, the machinists, and the engineers. Mr. Washington, would you care to say a few words?

WASHINGTON

I'm not much for politics, but yes, it's true.
We've come to an agreement. After all, we're
all Americans. And if it has to be war with
Germany—well then, we want to stand with
you, not against you.

ERNEST

An agreement? To join the Oligarchy? I have
heard these proposals before, they aim only to
take a few representatives of the union and make
them rich, at the cost of every other workman.
And have we turned away from war to turn back
to it again, just moments later? This is how the
Oligarchy destroys us from within. Soon every fit
workman in the United States will be possessed
by the ambition to become one of the favored, a
privileged leader. Thus will the strong men, who
might else be revolutionists, be won away and
their strength used to bolster the Oligarchy.

WICKSON

Your hour is done, Everhard. There will be no
more strikes.

ERNEST

No. In place of strikes will be slave revolts. And
you, Mr. Washington, you will become the chief
slave driver.

WICKSON

Do you see how he reveals his true aim? Not higher wages for the workers, but anarchy.

ERNEST

And what of the unskilled hands that Mr. Washington is supposed to represent but has sold for his own profit. How much were you offered Washington? And what is the offer to the workers? One cent or two cents, no more, and no more coming. Isn't that true?

WICKSON

So what do you propose instead? Revolution? Violence?

ERNEST

If necessary yes.

WICKSON

Whatever means necessary.

ERNEST

Yes. You yourself said—

WICKSON

You've had your time to speak. Now I think you should leave the speaking to your betters.

ERNEST

I will not be forced into silence!

(ROBERTS stands.)

ROBERTS

I would like a word or two if I might. It seems this debate has been dominated by two extreme views, as if those two views were the only alternative. But the Democratic Party has historically stood in a place of compromise, with one hand out to the worker, the other to those who seek to employ. There is no need to kowtow to the extremists—

(Suddenly, there is the sound of an explosion. And the world moves into slow motion.)

ANTONIA

Dear comrades, do I need to remind you of the bombings, 23 of them, all coordinated? Of the deaths, mostly among the Democrats? Of the arrests, the riots, the repercussions?

WICKSON

Anarchist! Anarchist!

ERNEST

It is a plot! Do nothing, or you will be destroyed!

AVIS

Then he slowly sank down, and the soldiers grabbed him. The next moment soldiers were everywhere, clearing the hall. I saw no more. I, too, was put under arrest. I heard of his trial, but did not witness it.

SCENE 14: THE TRIAL

ANTONIA

Here we must depend on a transcript of the trial.

ERNEST

I can say flatly, without qualification or doubt of any sort, that the Socialists had no hand in the affair. Who threw the bombs we do not know, but the one thing we are absolutely sure of is that we did not throw them.

ANTONIA

To which the judge responded, then whom do you blame for the crime, young man? You were witnessed calling for violence, just moments before the bomb was thrown. Some have theorized that you gave a signal, of sorts.

ERNEST

I was tricked into it. I believe the Iron Heel is responsible for the attack. Of course, I cannot prove this. But I believe that the Iron Heel planned and perpetrated the outrage for the purpose of foisting the guilt on our shoulders and so bringing about our destruction.

ANTONIA

That is a very serious accusation to make without evidence, the judge told him.

ERNEST

It is what I believe. It is the only explanation
I can find.

ANTONIA

Wickson testified as well.

WICKSON

It had been reported to the Speaker of the House,
by secret-service agents of the government, that
they had received rumors that the Socialists were
about to resort to terroristic tactics, and that the
Socialists had decided upon the day when their
tactics would go into effect. It was the very day of
the debate. I had been warned, and that was the
reason that so many soldiers were ready at the
call. How these terrorists were able to attack and
escape nonetheless I cannot say.

ERNEST

Isn't it obvious! If you were warned, and the hall
was full of soldiers, whom else but the Iron Heel
itself can have arranged this!

ANTONIA

The judge here reprimands Ernest for his behavior
in court and demands silence. Washington also
testified.

WASHINGTON

I saw him preparing something, in consultation with his Socialist brethren. They had approached me in the past about participating in their revolution, and I had avoided them. I am a believer in non-violence.

ERNEST

How much have you been paid?

ANTONIA

For this outburst, Ernest was removed. By the time the conviction came, it was a forgone conclusion. Guilty.

ACTOR

Was he?

ANTONIA

Was he what?

ACTOR

Guilty.

ANTONIA

No, of course not. The Black Hundreds must have done the deed, in service to the Oligarchy.

ACTOR

So that was later proved?

ANTONIA

No, the crime was never solved. But Avis said the same.

ACTOR

She loved him, of course.

ANTONIA

Yes.

ACTOR

So she would never believe him capable of such an act.

ANTONIA

What are you trying to say?

ACTOR

I was just wondering whether you thought it possible that the revolutionists were involved. Maybe not Everhard, but someone else within the party.

ANTONIA

It was one of the Black Hundreds. I am certain of it.

SCENE 15: THE ESCAPE

AVIS

Of myself, during this period, there is not much to say. For six months I was kept in prison, though charged with no crime. I was a suspect—a word of fear that all revolutionists were soon to come to know. But our own nascent secret service was beginning to work. By the end of my fourth month I was contacted by Joseph Parkhurst, the prison doctor, and a secret revolutionist.

PARKHURST

You will fain illness. Eventually, they will send you to the infirmary, and I will be your doctor. One of our network has asked to be transferred to the infirmary as well, he will be there to lead you to your escape.

AVIS

What of Ernest? If what I have heard about his trial is true, they will surely put him to death.

PARKHURST

Your job will be to find a secure hiding place. Ernest will join you when he can. There are over three hundred revolutionists currently in prison.

To succeed, we must try to release them all at once, otherwise it will lead to greater vigilance and suspicion. Remember, the jailers are workers too. Our main job now is to convert them to our cause.

AVIS

They are too entrenched.

PARKHURST

Some perhaps. Not all.

AVIS

It happened as he promised. Two nights into my stay at the infirmary, in the dead of night, a man whose name I never learned led me through the gates. He had new clothes, a new identity for me.

(As AVIS speaks, a MANSERVANT/ BIEDENBACH changes her clothes into that of a rich heiress.)

It was decided that I would be disguised as one of the daughters of a lesser oligarch, a man like Wickson, someone who wouldn't be questioned. I was accompanied by a manservant, Biedenbach by name. He was mostly silent, as he was German in origin, and suspicions of the Germans ran high. With the Oligarchs firmly in charge, the world stood once more at the brink of war.

BIEDENBACH

When I was a young man I was a soldier. It was
in Germany. There all young men must be in the
army. So I was in the army. There was another
soldier there, a young man, too. His father was
what you call an agitator, and his father was in
jail for lese majesty—what you call speaking the
truth about the Emperor.

AVIS

He was a socialist?

BIEDENBACH

Yes. German or American, we are brothers.
And sisters. This young man, he talked with me
much about people, and work, and the robbery
of the people by the capitalists. He made me
see things in new ways. When the cooperative
commonwealth comes, I will be glad.

AVIS

We traveled by train, then fishing boat. As
we drifted, I saw the lights of Alcatraz where
Ernest lay, and found comfort in the thought of
nearness to him. We reached San Pablo, then on
foot into the mountains of Sonoma. We settled in
an abandoned ranch.

BIEDENBACH

You must make yourself over again. You must cease to be. You must become another woman— and not merely in the clothes you wear, but inside your skin under the clothes. You must make yourself over again so that even your husband would not know you—your voice, your gestures, your mannerisms, your carriage, your walk, everything.

AVIS

But how will I live?

BIEDENBACH

I will come every week. More often if I can. I will bring you everything you need. Food, supplies. News of the outside, for I know it can be hard when you are in hiding.

AVIS

It's too dangerous a journey to try weekly.

BIEDENBACH

Remember, we are all brothers and sisters. I had a sister in Germany. I will probably never see her again. But you, I can help. I want to help.

AVIS

The news Biedenbach brought back was
often grim. One day, he told me my father
had disappeared. Our comrades sought him
everywhere. But he was lost as completely as if
the earth had swallowed him up. I spent months
weeping over his fate, even blaming Ernest for it.
But I also remembered how Ernest had tried to
protect my father, for my sake. It was not Ernest
who was to blame.

ANTONIA

Disappearance was one of the horrors of the
time. It was an inevitable concomitant of the
subterranean warfare that raged through those
three centuries. Without warning, without trace,
men and women, and even children, disappeared
and were seen no more, their end shrouded in
mystery.

SCENE 16: REUNION

AVIS

The wholesale jail delivery did not occur until well along into 1915. Complicated as it was, it was carried through without a hitch. From Cuba to California, hundreds of our leaders were released. There was not a single instance of miscarriage. Every one of them won to the refuges as planned. Yet when Ernest was at last led to my refuge, he did not know me.

(BIEDENBACH leads ERNEST to AVIS.)

BIEDENBACH

Please, wait here.

ERNEST

Where are you going? Where is my wife?

(BIEDENBACH exchanges a conspiratorial smile with AVIS.)

BIEDENBACH

You will have to wait for her, I suppose.

(BIEDENBACH exits.)

ERNEST

Do you know my Avis?

(AVIS nods.)

I did not know she had a companion here. I am grateful that you have kept her company, these last two years.

AVIS

Your wife has had no companions except for occasional visits from the German man who led you here.

ERNEST

Where is she then? I was led to believe this was her dwelling.

AVIS

It is.

ERNEST

Then who are you?

AVIS

Do you not recognize me at all, Ernest?

(ERNEST stares at her, then embraces her.)

ERNEST

It is as if I see two women. You are my Avis, and you are also someone else. You are my harem. At any rate, we are safe now. If the United States becomes too hot for us, why I have qualified for citizenship in Turkey.

ANTONIA

At the time, polygamy was practiced in Turkey.

AVIS

Eighteen months we spent together. Together, we built a house, and during that time artists, scientists, scholars, musicians and poets came to join us. In our hideout, culture was higher and finer than in the palaces and wonder cities of the oligarchs. For this was part of our fight. As one woman of our company sang, the proletariat did not need just bread, she needed roses too.

SONG: BREAD AND ROSES

COMPANY

As we come marching, marching
In the beauty of the day,
A million darkened kitchens,
A thousand mill lofts gray,
Are touched with all the radiance
That a sudden sun discloses,
For the people hear us singing:
"Bread and roses! Bread and roses!"

As we come marching, marching,
We battle too for men,
For they are women's children,
And we mother them again.
Our lives shall not be sweated
From birth until life closes;
Hearts starve as well as bodies;
Give us bread, but give us roses!

As we come marching, marching,
Unnumbered women dead
Go crying through our singing
Their ancient cry for bread.
Small art and love and beauty
Their drudging spirits knew.
Yes, it is bread we fight for—
But we fight for roses, too!

As we come marching, marching,
We bring the greater days.
And soon the revolution,
It will set the world ablaze
No more the drudge and idler—
Ten that toil where one reposes,
But a sharing of life's glories:
Bread and roses! Bread and roses!

SCENE 17: THE FATE OF BIEDENBACH

AVIS

Despite these moments of joy, those eighteen months were often difficult. Sometimes, I would think of all we had lost, would think of my father, and I would feel like I could barely breathe for the sadness. Ernest tried to understand but then became impatient. More losses followed, comrades who died or disappeared. The worst for me was when Biedenbach was shot and killed by one of our own lookouts, because he had forgotten the correct password.

ERNEST

Every day, when we were apart, I thought about seeing you, yet now you are hardly here. Is it Biedenbach?

AVIS

He was a good man. For two years, he kept me alive. Now they are calling him a traitor. There are rumors that he was shot for being a spy. It isn't true, Ernest.

ERNEST

How do you know? Maybe no one wanted to tell you that he betrayed us. Maybe they made up the story about the password, to comfort you.

AVIS

Because I knew him. I knew him, Ernest. Yes, he was sometimes absent minded, I can believe that lapse. But he was no traitor.

ERNEST

Some men are tempted by money.

AVIS

You know nothing about him!

ERNEST

You must remember the Cause, Avis. Whatever reason he died, it was in service of something bigger than either of us. Sometimes I feel like you forgot that while I was gone. When you're like this, I feel like this is that other woman I saw.

AVIS

What other woman?

ERNEST

The one who was here the day I returned, the one I did not recognize as being you until you told me.

AVIS

I am the same woman. But I am human. Allow me to mourn.

ANTONIA

Search as I might through all the material of those times that has come down to us, I can find no other mention of the fate of Biedenbach.

SCENE 18: THE TRAIN

AVIS

It was not until January, 1917, that we left
the refuge. All had been arranged, with fake
identities in place. I was supposed to be Ernest's
sister. Together, we took the train to Chicago.

ANTONIA

The city of Chicago was one of the storm-centres
of the conflict between labor and capital, a
city of street-battles and violent death, with a
class-conscious Capitalist organization and a
class-conscious workman organization. It is not
surprising, therefore, that Chicago also became
the storm-centre of the premature First Revolt.

ERNEST

The train has stopped.

AVIS

Perhaps it is a mechanical problem.

ERNEST

Perhaps. But in these times…

AVIS

Listen. Was that an explosion?

ERNEST

I did not hear it.

AVIS

There again. Closer.

ERNEST

That I heard. But how? The revolution is
months away.

CONDUCTOR

Everybody off the train! Everybody off the train!

AVIS

But we have not yet reached the station.

CONDUCTOR

Young woman, I would suggest you head
for safety. And quickly. The Revolutionists
are attacking.

SCENE 19: CHAOS IN CHICAGO

AVIS

We stepped off into chaos. People were running every which way, and plumes of smoke filled the sky. We headed for the great labor-ghetto on the South Side in the hope of getting in contact with some of the comrades. Too late! We knew it. A great screaming roar went up, dim with distance, punctuated with detonation after detonation. Turning the corner, we came upon a man. He was lying in a pool of blood.

(ERNEST examines DEAD MAN.)

ERNEST

Shot in the breast. Dead.

AVIS

One of ours?

ERNEST

He wears no uniform. I cannot say.

AVIS

How did this begin? No order had been given—

ERNEST

The Oligarchy. It must be. An agent must have
infiltrated, given the signal prematurely.

ACTOR

Was it the Oligarchy, Antonia?

ANTONIA

It must have been. Who else?

AVIS

Suddenly a change came over the face of
things. A tingle of excitement ran along the air.
Automobiles fled past, two, three, a dozen.

MAN ON STREET

Look out! Take cover!

ERNEST

Our brave comrades. They are coming.

(JACKSON enters, waving a gun.)

AVIS

Jackson!

(JACKSON shoots in their direction.
They dive for cover.)

Jackson! Don't you recognize us?

(JACKSON growls at them, takes another shot.)

What has happened to him?

ERNEST

He has lost his reason. He has become an
anarchist, or worse.

AVIS

Why? How?

ERNEST

There is no answer but to say that at such times
as these, men lose their souls. He has entered
the abyss, and he is glutting on vengeance. Keep
hidden, if he sees you he will kill you. His only aim
is death, now.

(JACKSON runs off.)

AVIS

The next moment a mob filled the street, an
awful river, the people of the abyss. Jackson
was not alone, he was just the forerunner.

I thought I had known the face of despair before, but now I found I was looking at it for the first time. It surged past my vision in concrete waves of wrath, snarling and growling, carnivorous, drunk with whiskey from pillaged warehouses, drunk with hatred, drunk with blood. Men, women, and children in rags and tatters, wan faces from which vampire society had sucked the juice of life, bloated forms swollen with physical corruption, festering youth and festering age, blasted with the ravages of disease and all the horrors of chronic innutrition—a raging, demonical horde.

(A CRAZED MAN launches himself at ERNEST. ERNEST stabs him and he falls to the ground.)

Who is he?

ERNEST

A dead man. That is all I know. Well, now I have killed. I am not sorry for it. It was necessary, even inevitable. But still. It is hard to be caught within the wheels of history.

(GARTHWAITE enters, and ERNEST swings towards him. GARTHWAITE holds his hand up.)

GARTHWAITE

Everhard, come with me.

ERNEST

Who are you? How do you know me?

GARTHWAITE

I am a comrade, and a friend. On a night like
tonight, it is hard to tell friend from foe. But I saw
you speak, years ago, and yours is a face I will
never forget. And who is she, your wife?

ERNEST

My sister.

GARTHWAITE

Very well, if you prefer. Your sister. We have a safe
house, not far.

ERNEST

If the revolution has come, I am ready to fight.

GARTHWAITE

The revolution has come. But look around you.
This battle is already lost.

ERNEST

The Oligarchy and their agents. We were not
ready. We were betrayed.

GARTHWAITE

Perhaps. And perhaps when a spark is lit, no one knows where the fire might spread. This fire has spread too far, too fast.

ERNEST

What now?

GARTHWAITE

Now we wait. This inferno may burn for hours, it may burn for days. But it will be put out. We will be blamed for the death and the damage. We will wait. We will try again.

AVIS

I didn't imagine it would be like this.

GARTHWAITE

Did you imagine one battle, simple and quick, and then victory?

(There is a roar of sound.)

ERNEST

Do you hear those screams? Where is that coming from?

GARTHWAITE

The asylum. The inmates must have escaped. Why not? The city has already gone mad.

AVIS

Bishop Morehouse!

ERNEST

What of him?

AVIS

That is where they sent him. Do you remember?

ERNEST

He has probably been sent on again and again since then.

AVIS

I must find him.

GARTHWAITE

There is no way you could reach him, even if he's there.

AVIS

Just then a bomb was dropped from the building above us. Garthwaite yelled a warning, and he and Earnest jumped inside the smashed window of a nearby store. I ran, leaving both behind. When I turned and looked behind me, I saw rubble. Somewhere within, I would come to learn, my husband and his comrade were traveling the only way available, down into the basement and from there through a series of catacombs under the city. My path led to the asylum.

And now a strange thing happened. A transformation came over me. The fear of death, for myself and for others, left me. I was strangely exalted, another being in another life. Nothing mattered. The Cause for this one time was lost, but the Cause would be here tomorrow, the same Cause, ever fresh and ever burning. And thereafter, in the orgy of horror that raged through the succeeding hours, I was able to take a calm interest. Death meant nothing, life meant nothing. I was an interested spectator of events, and, sometimes swept on by the rush, was myself a curious participant. For my mind had leaped to a star-cool altitude and grasped a passionless transvaluation of values. Had it not done this, I know that I should have died.

(She stumbles over a man. It may be the BISHOP.)

I do not know how many hours I stumbled among the dead and injured, through fire and bombs and madness. I finally came across a man, one of a pile of men. A familiar pair of shoulders in a cotton shirt and a familiar fringe of white hair caught my eye. His face had been blasted by a bomb. To this day I don't know if it was my Bishop, but as I held his hand, still warm, the world of my childhood flooded back to me. I waited, silent, unmoving, as the night filled with more cries, more fire. In the dawn, Ernest found me, still sitting.

(ERNEST approaches AVIS.)

ERNEST

Did you find him?

AVIS

If not him, another like him. Must all peaceful men die in this revolution?

ERNEST

I cannot say. Perhaps.

AVIS

Then I wonder if it is a revolution worth having, after all.

ERNEST

It is not our choice. The revolution must be fought, and our only choice is which side we will fight for.

AVIS

Or we can choose not to fight.

ERNEST

What would we have accomplished, then?

(The sound of a train whistle.)

Do you hear the train? The fighting has ended. The city has returned to its old tricks.

(The whistle repeats.)

AVIS

People are leaving?

ERNEST

Arriving. Slave-levies for the rebuilding of Chicago. You see, the Chicago slaves are all killed. They have to import more.

AVIS

The magnitude of what we faced then struck me. The only thing that sustained me was an idea, an idea that perhaps, maybe not in our lifetime but perhaps, there will be a society where—

(AVIS stops.)

CODA

ACTOR

Where what?

(ANTONIA comes forward.)

ANTONIA

The manuscript ends there. But she obviously means our society, what else?

AVIS

Are there any clues as to what happened to her, after?

ANTONIA

Nothing but what she wrote at the beginning of her story.

ACTOR

That must have been fifteen years later.

ANTONIA

Yes, about that long.

ERNEST

And Ernest?

ANTONIA

We know he died for his part in the Second Revolt. Other than that, we know no more.

ACTOR

How did Ernest die?

ANTONIA

He was executed, I am sure. Though we have not yet found a transcript of that trial.

ACTOR

Then how do you know?

ANTONIA

It is the logic of history.

ACTOR

He could have died so many different ways. Maybe through a fellow revolutionary's mistake, like Biedenbach. Or by the hand of someone gone mad, like Jackson's victims. Or the victim of a stray bomb, like the Bishop. How do we know it is by execution?

ERNEST

It was by execution. It must have been. He was the hero.

AVIS

One of many heroes.

ACTOR

Are there no other mentions of him?
You must have found something, in your
work as a historian and propagandist.

ANTONIA

There is a song. I think you know it. There
is an account I read of a great meeting of
revolutionaries. Avis and Ernest were both listed
as attending. The account states it ended with
this song, a sort of anthem. It was written before
the real revolution began, at the end of the
nineteenth century. It was as if they could see into
the future, see the struggles of the revolution, see
through the centuries all the way to today. It is
called "The Red Flag", for that was the color of the
banner that they waved, the same color as the flag
in the capital today. Comrades, will you join me
and sing it together?

SONG: THE RED FLAG
(The tune is "O Tannenbaum")

COMPANY

The people's flag is deepest red,
It shrouded oft our martyred dead,
And ere their limbs grew stiff and cold,
Their hearts' blood dyed its every fold.

Chorus:
Then raise the scarlet standard high.
Within its shade we'll live and die,
Though cowards flinch and traitors sneer,
We'll keep the red flag flying here.

Look round, the Frenchman loves its blaze,
The sturdy German chants its praise,
In Moscow's vaults its hymns were sung
Chicago swells the surging throng.

Chorus:
Then raise the scarlet standard high.
Within its shade we'll live and die,
Though cowards flinch and traitors sneer,
We'll keep the red flag flying here.

It waved above our infant might,
When all ahead seemed dark as night;
It witnessed many a deed and vow,
We must not change its color now.

Chorus:
Then raise the scarlet standard high.
Within its shade we'll live and die,
Though cowards flinch and traitors sneer,
We'll keep the red flag flying here.

With head uncovered swear we all
To bear it onward till we fall;
Come dungeons dark or gallows grim,
This song shall be our parting hymn.

Chorus:
Then raise the scarlet standard high.
Within its shade we'll live and die,
Though cowards flinch and traitors sneer,
We'll keep the red flag flying here.

www.ingramcontent.com/pod-product-compliance
Lightning Source LLC
Chambersburg PA
CBHW060125260626
47160CB00005B/2027